THE EAST MIDLANDS

First published in Great Britain in 2010 by
Young Writers, Remus House, Coltsfoot Drive,
Peterborough, PE2 9JX
Tel (01733) 890066 Fax (01733) 313524
Website: www.youngwriters.co.uk

Disclaimer
Young Writers has maintained every effort
to publish stories that will not cause offence.
Any stories, events or activities relating to individuals
should be read as fictional pieces and not construed
as real-life character portrayal.

Foreword

Since Young Writers was established in 1990, our aim
has been to promote and encourage written creativity
amongst children and young adults. By giving aspiring
young authors the chance to be published, Young Writers
effectively nurtures the creative talents of the next generation,
allowing their confidence and writing ability to grow.

With our latest fun competition, *The Adventures Starts
Here …* , secondary school children nationwide were
given the tricky challenge of writing a story with a
beginning, middle and an end in just fifty words.

The diverse and imaginative range of entries made the
selection process a difficult but enjoyable task with stories
chosen on the basis of style, expression, flair and technical
skill. A fascinating glimpse into the imaginations of the future,
we hope you will agree that this entertaining collection
is one that will amuse and inspire the whole family.

Contents

The Mini Sagas

Untitled

A couple buy a puppy. It wrecks the house and gets into tons of trouble. They have children, and are thinking of getting rid of him, but the man won't let them. In the end the dog dies. All the family are upset but they keep the memories in them.

Michaela Goldring (13)
De Aston School, Market Rasen

1

Again?

It was strange walking through the woods. I came across an old, deserted house. It was dark inside, with cobwebs. A sudden noise came from upstairs. 'Hello?' I said. No reply.
Another noise in the opposite room. I went in. 'Boo!' she screamed aloud. 'I love hide-and-seek! Again?'

Jenny Hunter (14)
De Aston School, Market Rasen

Trying To Hide

It's coming, it's coming back; I can't stop it, it won't work, it never does. I can't bear it, I've tried to run, but it's everywhere. Nobody understands, nobody really knows, nobody really cares. I really have to get out of here, I hate it; the dreaded day of Christmas.

Nancy Bibby (13)
De Aston School, Market Rasen

The Great Riot!

After the extraordinary match between the great derby of Grimsby Town and Lincoln City, a massive riot broke out. Fists were flying like darts in mid-air! Legs were being thrown around like cricket balls being thrown! Finally the police arrived and calmed down the riot and the angered fans.

Tony Hanson (13)

De Aston School, Market Rasen

A Day Of Adventure!

Wonderful green, hilly landscape! Then the sky turned grey; a storm started. Earthquakes happened and repeated. Birds that were ten times the size of him attacked. He screamed and hid. The sun came out, earthquakes stopped and he carried on moving. Then the snail reached the end of the leaf.

Carly Mason (14)

De Aston School, Market Rasen

Running

I was running. It felt like I was king of the world. The breeze through my hair, the birds tweeting, the squelch from under my feet. I tripped over into a pile of … ahh. I looked around, it was only a dream, but what's on my face? Well, you guess …

Joe Smedley (13)

De Aston School, Market Rasen

Untitled

As I walk over to him, my frown transforms into a
smile; my childhood dream has become reality.
You know when he's coming by the sound of new
shoes. Your heart melts with affection when you
look into his gentle brown eyes. I love my horse.

Bethany Sharpe (13)
De Aston School, Market Rasen

7

Troublesome Sandwiches

Apprehension filled me as I set off to the unit. I was filling with guilt as I walked down the corridor. I thought to myself, *Lord, what have I done now?* The unit doors opened in front of me; and there was my mum saying, 'You forgot your lunch dear.'

Jack Evans (14)
De Aston School, Market Rasen

Freedommmmmmmm!

I'm swimming … I'm walking … I'm running … I'm flying … I want to be an explorer. I just want to be free. The beautiful coral reefs … The coral shimmering and bubbling with life though they're so still. I'm swimming … I'm walking … I'm running … I'm falling … I'm flying … I'm exploring … Yes, I'm *free!*

Martha Poole (12)

De Aston School, Market Rasen

9

The Never-Ever Smile

The mystery walked down the street, running
slowly. With a sad frown it grinned. The smile was
so deep it made people cry with anger. Nobody
could see this highly visible frown. It stretched
from ear to ear happily. The price was high for
this majestic smile, small.

Maia Folger (12)

De Aston School, Market Rasen

Fluffy Stuff

I'd just come from Mars; never seen all this fluffy
stuff. Walking in Skegness, seeing it all around,
kids pointing at them; looking mesmerised,
wanting to pick it themselves. Begging parents,
'Please Mum, please!' I'm wondering what it is. It
can be made at home - it's only candyfloss.

Damon Brumpton (14)
De Aston School, Market Rasen

The Fat Man Asteroid

Our enemy; Fat Man. He wanted to be an
astronaut but fitness … He lives on a vertical hill.
It took me an hour to get up. I set a bag on fire
and ran. He came out shocked. Tripped and went
into the Earth. The Fat Man asteroid.

Thomas Steer (13)

De Aston School, Market Rasen

12

Mystery Footstep

There's an old derelict house in Greenwood Forest. Shane went to investigate. Suddenly he heard footsteps and creaks. Sweat ran down his forehead as he ran towards the door. They got closer, he was terrified. 'How much is the price, Sir?'

'100,000 is the price, Sir.'

'I'll take it, thanks!'

Sophie Frith (13)

De Aston School, Market Rasen

Untitled

It was a dark night, glooming with mist. Fred was in the kitchen when he heard a noise coming from upstairs. It was only the cat on the ledge! Then he heard a slam. It was the door. Then all of a sudden he could hear noises behind him. 'Surprise!'

Liam Rounce (13)

De Aston School, Market Rasen

Manhunt

The marines hid as bullets ricocheted off the wall.
The marines ducked and took cover from the fire.
Jack, a courageous soldier, stood up and sprayed
bullets at the enemy. A shot was fired and a bullet
flew through his head! Everyone gasped as the
game ended.

Kain Stones (14)
De Aston School, Market Rasen

15

The Huge Fish

Greg sat there in his green bivvy surrounded by his equipment. It was a miserable day. Suddenly there was a buzz, then another. He could hear line screaming off the reel. He grabbed the rod, struck into a huge fish. He landed the 40lb mirror carp. It was huge.

Gregory Fussey (13)
De Aston School, Market Rasen

Little Red Riding Hood

Once, a little girl called Little Red Riding Hood was happily walking through the woods to see her nan. When she got there she noticed how big her nan's eyes and nose were. It was the wolf. As the wolf jumped for her, she stabbed him in the heart.

Gemma Green (14)
De Aston School, Market Rasen

Running For Your Life

She ran through the woods, not stopping to take one breath. She could hear the footsteps behind her. She tried to run faster, but she was getting too tired. She tripped then fell to the ground. He was coming. He knelt to the ground and whispered, 'Tag, you're it!'

Jade Clarke

De Aston School, Market Rasen

He's Catching Me

Dave was running for his life. It was now or never.
He looked over his shoulder. He was catching up,
getting closer and closer. Dave was so scared, he
just ran and ran. He was so close, so near. He just
had to run. 'Yes!' He had won the race.

Joshua McCabe (14)
De Aston School, Market Rasen

Dragon?

One day a young boy went outside and saw fire coming out of a cave. He decided to climb up to the top. He explored the dark, gloomy cave; he spotted movement in the corner … He edged closer to find a huge, tall, menacing, ginger family, whimpering in the shadows.

Elliott Moden (13)

De Aston School, Market Rasen

Untitled

I walked through the door, I shouted, 'Tristen!'
No answer. I shouted again when I felt a sudden
drop of water on my nose. I ran upstairs and
shouted, 'What are … ' I gasped. Tristen was lying
in the bath, blood running over the side. He was
dead.

Charlotte Emmerson (12)
De Aston School, Market Rasen

A Science Lesson In Fairy Land!

It was a bubbly jubbly day in Fairy Land, the microscopic fairies were experimenting with pixie dust. Miss Mokerina was screaming at the devious fairy: Mildred. Why? Mildred had selfishly stolen the magnificent shimmering Tipp-Ex! But little did they know that Angelena used the wrong acid; and that was that!

Ciara Dodd (12)

De Aston School, Market Rasen

Jack's Footsteps

It was a sunny day. Suddenly I heard footsteps
from somebody called Jack. Next I said to him,
'What are you doing, evil person?'
Jack said, 'I just wanted a friend because I have
fallen out with Olivia, my best friend.'
In the end we all lived happily ever after.

Brandon Phillips (12)
De Aston School, Market Rasen

23

The Dodgy Dude

There was a man, he was a psycho. He ran around breaking cars and shooting. The man was careless one day. He was in pursuit of a SWAT van carrying a VIP, but the man got hit by the SWAT van. They thought they'd killed him, but he got up.

Freddie Fenwick (13)

De Aston School, Market Rasen

Shannon In The Deep, Dark Wood

There once was a girl called Shannon. She loved
to go for a walk through the deep, dark wood.
One day, while she was on her morning stroll, a
big bad wolf came and kidnapped her. Shannon
was never to be seen again. Her family was very
upset.

Ella Lee (12)

De Aston School, Market Rasen

25

Fall Down For Great Parties

We were dancing like mad to our favourite song of all time. The lights dimmed, the music was loud. Everyone was minding their own business. Suddenly everyone stopped and laughed. What were they all laughing at? Wait, I think I know - yes, my shorts were not where they should be.

Melissa Bett (14)

De Aston School, Market Rasen

Stalking The Prey

As I was walking I found myself hungry, so I wanted something juicy and chewy. Then I struck gold: a whole herd of deer. I couldn't believe my eyes. I crept up and ... *got you!* I ripped it to shreds and it was lovely, it was too good to share.

Alice Simpson (13)

De Aston School, Market Rasen

He, My Man

I wandered through the woods on a dark night, wondering if I'd see him again. *Crunch,* went the leaves under my feet; I made my way through the thorns. Suddenly a gigantic wolf popped out of nowhere, chasing me like thunder! Then he, my man in silver armour, saved me!

Shannon-Louise Thomas (13)

De Aston School, Market Rasen

Boxing

There was a boxer who was inadequate. He met Muhammad Ali. He said, 'These gloves will make you the best boxer in history.' He tried them in his next match and was victorious. He became sixth time world champion and beat Mike Tyson seven times. He is the best.

Aidan Bell (13)
De Aston School, Market Rasen

Nick The Lover Boy

There was a boy called Nick. He loved a girl, but she didn't love him. Nick didn't know this until his best friend told him. He was so upset! His friend didn't know what to do. He found a new girl in the end. She was beautiful. They got married.

Phoebe Alexandra Robertson (14)

De Aston School, Market Rasen

The Haunted House And The Boys!

On the day of today exactly 100 years ago, three boys went into a castle and according to their parents, they were never seen again. Legend has it they were eaten by vicious monsters (ghosts). You see they went into the castle at 16.30pm … 24 hours later, never seen again!

Fleur Rachel Callaway (13)

De Aston School, Market Rasen

Snow White

There once was a girl called Snow White and she ran away because her stepmum was going to kill her. She met these seven dwarves and they looked after her until her stepmum found out and poisoned her with an apple. Then the prince had to kiss her lips.

Lauren Knowles (14)
De Aston School, Market Rasen

Little Red Riding Hood

There was a girl who wore a red cloak. She took some cakes in a basket to her grandma. But she went through the woods. When she got there it wasn't her grandma in bed, it was a wolf that tried to eat her. A woodcutter cut off his head.

Shannon White (13)

De Aston School, Market Rasen

Robert's Trip To The Hospital

William saw Robert at hospital. Robert was in
hospital. A doctor came in, 'What's the problem?'
Robert said, 'My leg's broken.' The doctor
directed him to a room. He put Robert in the
strap and started sawing away. Robert yelled like
a lion in pain. He laughed and ran off.

William Turner (12)

De Aston School, Market Rasen

Rabbiting

One dark night me and my friend went shooting near a farm. There were a lot of rabbits. Every time we turned the lamp on, they all ran away. We turned the lamp off, waited a minute, loaded the guns, turned the lamp on and had a quick shot.

Jolon Mallinson (13)

De Aston School, Market Rasen

35

Phantom Of Cornwall

Each Christmas at Penryn, in Cornwall, England, a phantom coach, drawn by headless horses, is said to appear. But everyone who has seen the sight has vanished from the face of the Earth within a few hours. This strange sighting has happened ever since 1880 and will probably not stop ...

Harry Weatherall (12)
De Aston School, Market Rasen

36

Birds Of Death

Once upon a time a man wandered through the ghostly forest. At the same time, a flock of hummingbirds flew through the air. They circled him. As they did it made a multicoloured band and then it got closer and closer until they weren't further than a few feet …

Callum Darling (12)

De Aston School, Market Rasen

Sasha's Dancing Dream

Sasha stared at the dancers. *Wish I could be one!* The teacher caught her watching, 'Come try.' 'OK,' she said, quietly walking to the girls. She started clumsily but soon got into it, gracefully twirling with ease. She soon became professional and danced across the world. 'I'm so happy!'

Tasha Darby (13)

De Aston School, Market Rasen

38

Kyle's Farm

I live on a farm. I love sheep, they say *baa, baa*.
On Kyle's farm I have a dog, he goes *woof, woof*.
On Kyle's farm I have a tractor, it goes *honk, honk*.
On Kyle's farm it sounds like; *baa, baa, woof, woof,*
honk, honk, on Kyle's farm.

Kyle Beal (12)
De Aston School, Market Rasen

Me, Myself And I

It was a dark night striding through the forest, I suddenly saw something. All I knew was it was so horrific. The disgusting smell surrounded me. It was a body! I screamed and turned and felt an excruciating pain. I was dead, and now I know the body was mine.

Dominique Fieldsend (13)

De Aston School, Market Rasen

Dave And The Cow Crew

There was once a band called DATCC. They had a concert on in London. Everyone was going to see them, but I couldn't because I was skint. I could hear the head-banging tunes in my bedroom.

The next day at school everyone was bragging and singing the songs.

Tom Crawford (13)

De Aston School, Market Rasen

41

Mental Cinderella

Cinderella had two sisters and one day she killed them. Then she went to the ball and killed everyone. Her slipper dropped off. DCI Prince found it and tried the shoe on everyone. When he found Cinderella he took her to prison to get the electric chair.

Gregory Reynolds (13)
De Aston School, Market Rasen

The Message

Young boy sits in golden sunset, awaiting its arrival. Wing beats fill the blood sky. The talons hit the floor. The black-blue cloak sparkles in the sun. The boy stands and approaches the animal. The animal stays still … gets the note … opens it … It reads … 'Tea's ready, love Mum'.

Megan Goodyear (14)
De Aston School, Market Rasen

43

The Tiger

I lay down, hidden in the long stalks of grass. I was hungry. Then two rabbits hopped into the field and stopped to eat some grass. And there I lay, waiting to pounce. I bent my knees, bared my teeth, jumped and both of the rabbits were gone.

Celine Worrall (14)

De Aston School, Market Rasen

The Job

As the man approached the house with the old decaying walls, he couldn't help but notice the corpse of a mouse next to the cold stone path. The man couldn't stop as he had a job to do. The man knocked three times and waited for his sister to come.

Kieran Westwick (13)

De Aston School, Market Rasen

45

Alice Is Dead!

In Wonderland there lived Rabbit. He woke up from a deep sleep and found Alice was dead. He went underground, fought with Caterpillar and went through a door. On the other side, Mad Hatter tried to kill him, but Rabbit drank a bottle that turned him big! *Stomp!*

Chloe Depledge (12)
De Aston School, Market Rasen

A Nasty Encounter

'Argh!' Chris hurtled through the air at what felt to him like a million miles per hour. *Crunch!* He landed on something hairy and soft. As he opened his eyes, he saw a huge tongue surrounded by razor-sharp teeth. He shouted desperately for help, but it was too late …

Thomas Brocklebank

De Aston School, Market Rasen

Midnight Sun!

Love at first sight. Edward and Bella were in love. For Bella's birthday she got a stereo for her truck and tickets to Florida. Esmé bought them a house. Bella became pregnant with a little girl. They called her Renesmé but the Volturi wanted her dead. Renesmé won the battle!

Courtney Anne Baxter (12)
De Aston School, Market Rasen

The Kiss Of A Frog Prince

Once upon a time there lived a beautiful princess.
Everyone in the kingdom loved her, but the only
person she loved was her pet frog!
One day she was talking to her pet, when
suddenly the frog jumped on her and kissed her
on the lips, turning into a prince!

Tonicha Watson (13)

De Aston School, Market Rasen

Untitled

Goldilocks went into the strange house, she munched the porridge, broke the chairs and slept in the beds. When the owners got home, Daddy and Mummy Bear said, 'Who's been eating our porridge, broken our chairs and slept in our beds?'
'Never mind that,' said Baby, 'who's nicked the TV?'

Callum Codd

De Aston School, Market Rasen

Chloe's Last Ride

Once there was a girl called Chloe. She liked roller coasters. There was one called 13! As she stepped on, a ghostly howl made her shiver. She was shivering as she was strapped in. The ride started. Chloe looked to her side, screamed, and that was her last ride!

Adele Ibbitson (12)

De Aston School, Market Rasen

Little Red Riding Hood With A Twist

There was a girl called Red, she always wore a red hood. There was someone stealing goodies, so she took her recipes to Granny, where she found a wolf disguised as Granny, Granny tied up and a woodcutter with an axe. But it was the bunny's fault from the start!

Elisabeth Davidson (12)

De Aston School, Market Rasen

The Gumdrop Fountain

A long time ago, in a land far away, lived a
leprechaun dancing in a tree. Short but sharp,
he fell from the tree and landed in a gumdrop
fountain. He got hit on the head with a gumdrop
and fainted. Needless to say, Santa pulled him out
to safety.

Abigail Hebert (13)
De Aston School, Market Rasen

The Eruption

The sky turns dark, not a cloud to be seen. The
ground shakes in horror. Screams can be heard
from villages afar. Bright orange lava pours out
from a black cloud of smoke. The population flees
to safety and the mammals run to the sea. The
mighty volcano roars again!

Rebecca Dame

De Aston School, Market Rasen

Bob's Zombie Madness

One day everyone turned to horrible zombies, apart from Bob. Bob was running away when he saw a helicopter on a roof and a shotgun with ammo on the floor. He decided to kill as many zombies as he could and take it to the helicopter. Then he left, forever!

Jared Gibson

De Aston School, Market Rasen

The Shop

Jim was walking down the narrow, dirty street. He looked uneasily at one of the shops. He opened the old, crusty door with a creak. Taking a step into the shop, the floorboards squeaking as he shifted his weight, he avidly looked around. There it was! The new code!

Axel Schygiol (13)
De Aston School, Market Rasen

Gang Wars

In a time when two rival gangs were fighting for power. The gangs were Black Hawks and White Falcons. They were fighting down the local park. The gangs had knives and baseball bats. The Falcons stabbed the Hawks and the leader gave in. The White Falcons had all the power.

Josh Feetham (12)

De Aston School, Market Rasen

57

Reality Check!

Taya stood facing the dreaded beast, hands
clenched with a burning ball of fire. The beast
glared at her, its eyes looking straight through her.
'Tayla, pass the ball!' Stevie shouted as Taya came
back into reality. She passed the ball to Stevie. She
jumped, she shot, she scored! *Yay!*

Kelsey Snowden (12)
De Aston School, Market Rasen

The Man And The Van

There once was a man called Bill. He saw an ambulance, so he chased after it. The ambulance went faster, but Bill caught up with it. They finally stopped and waited for Bill to arrive. When he got there, he said, 'I'd like a Coke and an ice cream please.'

Harrison Cattell (13)

De Aston School, Market Rasen

Ingo

Ingo is lonely at night. The darkness is closed all around me, but I'm not alone. Faro is somewhere. He's here, he's just hiding. Now it's cold and I'm afraid. I don't know where I am. The water hates me, it wants to destroy me. Where is Ingo? 'Help!'

Lucy Coles (12)

De Aston School, Market Rasen

My One And Only

I could do nothing but stand still. He was the most beautiful thing I'd ever seen. He had the most amazing dark complexion, he even smelled gorgeous. I was now drooling. I couldn't resist; I bit straight into him. He was the best cheeseburger I've ever had in my life!

Megan Jannette Hartle Johnson (14)

De Aston School, Market Rasen

The Werewolf

I saw a figure move in the moonlight. I got scared. Then a werewolf jumped onto me. I punched it in the face. I quickly pulled my penknife out and stabbed it. Tumbling down the hill, I got home and heard a cry from the top of the misty hill.

Joseph Fraser Watson (13)
Mount St Mary's College, Spinkhill

The Robbery

'How's this gonna happen?' Tommy was anxious.
'We're gonna blow through the back and straight
to the vault,' explained Charlie confidently. *Boom!*
They were in! Unfortunately they didn't expect a
cloud of blue dye to blow out of the walls. They
grabbed the money and drove off, police speeding
after.

Marcus Read (14)

Mount St Mary's College, Spinkhill

63

Ace Ventura

A dolphin gets stolen and there is only one man to solve the mystery. The dolphin belongs to one of America's most famous football teams. Ace retrieves the dolphin and watches the big football final. The team go on and win the football final grand slam. Ace receives a prize.

Charlie Walsham (14)

Mount St Mary's College, Spinkhill

Love

Small town high school girl never met her true love until she laid eyes on the coolest boy in her school. They both got lost in each other's eyes. Now that she's his girlfriend, she finds being popular isn't all that great, but still wants to keep her relationship strong.

Amy Lavin (13)
Mount St Mary's College, Spinkhill

The Narrow Passage

We crept deviously to a narrow passage between the thorn bushes. We had never been here before. We sneakily got through a gap in the bush at the end of the alley. I shut my eyes, aware of the thorns, launched myself through the prickly hole and gasped to see …

Hannah Parsons (13)

Mount St Mary's College, Spinkhill

The Plane Wreck

The sound of the engines roaring, my ears pop.
I fall asleep. I wake up to the sound of shouting
and thunder, wailing and screaming as the plane
plummets. The plane shakes, everything goes
dark.
I wake and shriek. The water is rising. I see a
fireball flying towards me …

James Hill (13)
Mount St Mary's College, Spinkhill

67

The Terrible Disaster

The wind picked up and caught my sails, ramming
me into the rocks, ripping the side of my boat
into the raging sea. We sent a message for help,
but there was no reply. My crew, surviving on
very little food and warm clothing, started to
starve and get hypothermia.

James Barker (13)
Mount St Mary's College, Spinkhill

Shipwrecked

Crack! The storm blew through the ripped sails of the smashed boat. Towards the ship, the cold chilled my bones. Squeezing through the damaged hull was difficult, but it was nothing to what I saw inside. The sight was horrific, it made me vomit. Dead bodies all over the floor.

Ben White (14)

Mount St Mary's College, Spinkhill

69

Final Countdown

There's about ten seconds of the third period in the Stanley Cup Final. Crosby gets one more chance to go on a break away. He goes in and out of the defence. Only three seconds before the buzzer, he takes the shot - goal - and that seals a win for Pittsburg.

Guy Swales (15)
Mount St Mary's College, Spinkhill

The Beast

Excitedly we set off to a rock concert in our ancient VW Camper, rattling violently as we turned off the main road. 'Where are we?' The map was gone, so was Dave … We got scared. The destructive beast hunted us and devoured us all, leaving blood and guts sprayed everywhere.

Daniel Hodkin (13)

Mount St Mary's College, Spinkhill

Last Over

Siddle runs in (after two England drinks breaks)
and bowls. *Bang!* Ohioas hits the ball into the
ground like he has done for the last five balls.
Ricky Ponting looks at the clock for the last time.
Walks towards Anderson and it's over. England
draw the game.

Joe Tetley (14)
Mount St Mary's College, Spinkhill

Cinderella

Cinderella is a poor servant who works for her sisters. Cinderella is sad because she wants to go to a ball because she's always working. Her fairy godmother grants her wish to go to the ball. She marries the boy who dances with her at the ball.

Shumila Hassan (14)
Mount St Mary's College, Spinkhill

73

The Hangover

Four brave men go drinking at a wedding.
The next morning they wake up to find their best
friend Doug is missing. They search everywhere
for him. Strange clues lead them in the wrong
direction, but they forget to look in the most
obvious place.

Matthew Woodcock-Fowles (14)

Mount St Mary's College, Spinkhill

Crack

Crack. Egg everywhere. The king's men were all confused. He lay there next to the wall severely battered and bruised, cracked egg everywhere. The king nearly blew a fuse. Cracked egg everywhere - Humpty-Dumpty was not amused!

James Wilkinson (14)

Mount St Mary's College, Spinkhill

75

The Turtle And The Rabbit

Once there was a turtle and rabbit in a forest.
One day the rabbit challenged the turtle because
he was slow. The turtle accepted.
Second day the rabbit and turtle had a race. The
turtle won because the rabbit was shot in the leg
and was disqualified.

Wilson Hsu (12)

Mount St Mary's College, Spinkhill

The Two Little Kittens

Once there were two kittens, Misha and Mittens. When they were born their owners killed their mum and left the kittens in a cardboard box in the snow for two days, until the RSPCA took them for recovery. They got given to me and my next-door neighbour. Yay!

Emily Miles (12)
Mount St Mary's College, Spinkhill

SOS Alert

Thousands of miles away from Britain, was a stranded traveller. He had crash-landed on a sandbank. The only food and drinks were water and five biscuits. He broke some of the wing off and made a raft then after he built the raft he sent a flare for help.

George Collins (12)

Mount St Mary's College, Spinkhill

The Story Of EastEnders

I walked into the room of my jail cell. I was
shocked. I was sent down for murder. I killed
Archie Mitchell again, and no, it wasn't Stacey
Slater this time! But the Bulgarians have eaten his
body and my sniper, that killed him, is on auction
for millions.

Jordan Falding (12)
Mount St Mary's College, Spinkhill

Born To Run

It was mysterious walking through the park, I was scared. My dog had run away when I was walking him here. He wouldn't respond. *He was so quick, he could be a race dog,* I thought. I couldn't find him, I saw him though, racing on TV, what a dog!

Harry Chapman
Mount St Mary's College, Spinkhill

The Factory Of Death!

It was about midnight. Molly walked into the factory. It was a very dark, gloomy place. As she began to walk further into the factory she heard a creak, which made her jump. It turned out to be the floorboards. She began to jog, then *bang!* She was dead!

Elliot Bounds (13)

Mount St Mary's College, Spinkhill

Soup Of Creation

Darren stepped forward into the soup of creation with a huge splash. The green liquid melted his skin. He tried to scream in pain, but he had no lips. The liquid went into his lungs. It melted his internal organs as his hollow bones slowly drifted to the deep pit.

James Oliver (12)
Mount St Mary's College, Spinkhill

Untitled

Ellie walked into her house. It was dark and gloomy. She was scared as she walked into the living room. She screamed. Dead bodies everywhere. Her mum, dad, brother, sister; *dead!* There was blood pouring everywhere. There was a knock at the door! *Knock … knock … knock …* *'Argh!'*

Olivia Smith (13)
Mount St Mary's College, Spinkhill

83

Millie

Millie walked into the house hearing weird noises in her kitchen. She entered the kitchen, finding her mum with a puppy in her hands which her mum was going to cook for tea.

Kiran Kaur (13)

Mount St Mary's College, Spinkhill

Untitled

Sophie walked into a graveyard. It was old, scary, dark and haunted. She heard a scream and a snap as if someone snapped a branch. Sophie was that scared she wet herself, and Diesel the dog was scared, so he hid between her legs, so she peed on him.

Hannah Hallam (13)

Mount St Mary's College, Spinkhill

The Theatre

The old cracked door to the ghostly theatre
slid open revealing the darkness within. The
floorboards creaked under my weight. Clouds of
dust rained down on my head as I approached the
second set of ancient doors. The floor gave way
to darkness.

Bradley Brooks (12)

Mount St Mary's College, Spinkhill

Just Kiran Kaur

Kiran walked up the stairs following the screams that came from her room. She went up the creaky stairs step by step. She grabbed hold of the door handle dreading what was inside. She pushed the door open and saw her mum playing with a guinea pig, happily.

Millie Boot (13)
Mount St Mary's College, Spinkhill

87

Death

It was dark, very dark. Dan had been misled. He was told to come here on the stroke of midnight. He turned to leave, but something stopped him. He was being watched. He turned to leave. The sight shocked him. He saw blood - his blood. He didn't draw another breath.

Oliver Gavins (13)

Mount St Mary's College, Spinkhill

Mandy's Revenge

The mist of darkness, the stench of the pond, and the fear of Jimmy, all made Mandy's revenge plan more exciting! Mandy was calling Jimmy on his phone, asking him to come outside. He was walking outside, he walked into the string and fell over into the pond. *Splash, plop!*

Hollie Woodhead (13)
Mount St Mary's College, Spinkhill

89

The Fall

His big shoe caught the rope laid out by the people he thought his friends. He collapsed onto the floor. Luckily his padded stomach broke his fall. His nose was big, red and round, and his hair was a curly mess. Getting to his feet the clown took a bow.

Hannah Steed (13)

Mount St Mary's College, Spinkhill

The Dark

It was dark. There were all sorts of monsters popping out from everywhere, all of their grotesque faces leering at me. I was scared. I didn't know what was happening to me. I started to slow down. I thought they were going to get me. Then the ghost ride finished.

Joseph Skull (12)

Mount St Mary's College, Spinkhill

91

The Angry Ocean

The thunder boomed angrily. The boat bobbed about on the towering waves on the vast ocean. The moon shone down with a mysterious gleam. The boat sank further as water gushed into its hold. The wind huffed. Lightning crackled. Waves crashed. The boat drifted silently down to the ocean floor.

Sophie McMurray (13)
Mount St Mary's College, Spinkhill

Closer Universe

You could hear her panting from the valley. Her heart was racing. She was being chased! It was getting closer and closer then she fell into the cold, still river.
A week later and nobody knew anything. Little did they know she'd passed through to the universe parallel to ours.

Olivia Cristinacce-Travis (13)

Mount St Mary's College, Spinkhill

93

The Big Mess

She knelt down on the floor cleaning it all up.
'God, that boy is really messy. I hope he gets
cleaner. Imagine what his girlfriend would say
when she comes round. She might even dump
him. That'll teach him. I need a word with him
when he gets back!

Thomas Czyszczon-Burton (13)
Mount St Mary's College, Spinkhill

The Fall

Darkness descended upon Jack like a black veil.
Lights glittered and twinkled around him, dancing
in the twilight glow. Suddenly, without warning,
Jack fell. He kept on plummeting, but when he
opened his mouth to scream, no sound was
uttered. Abruptly, out of nowhere, a threatening
growl pierced the air ...

William Daly (13)
Mount St Mary's College, Spinkhill

95

The Insolent Submarine-Drawing Child

'Is that a bottom you are drawing in your exercise book?' he boomed.

'No, Mister Morris, it's a submarine,' he said.

'Well draw a bottom then! This is biology, not art!' The teacher took a deep breath, only to be interrupted by the insolent child.

'Go away!' he muttered rudely.

Harry Castle (12)

Mount St Mary's College, Spinkhill

The Babysitter

Yesterday was a dark gloomy night, John arrived
back home, his parents were away in France and
his babysitter was supposed to look after him.
As he walked in he could just see him sitting on
a chair, with a knife. He was waiting for John,
waiting to kill him.

Sam Bowler (13)
Mount St Mary's College, Spinkhill

Too Late

Her heart felt like it had been ripped out of her chest. Tears streamed down her mascara-streaked face. Why did he do this to her? She ran on through the rain, heart beating, feet pounding on the ground. She saw the car before she could move. Too late - *screech!*

Emily Morley (13)
Mount St Mary's College, Spinkhill

The Angry Lord President

The Lord President entered the Time Lord
council chamber. 'Where has Davros positioned
his Dalek squads?' he demanded.
'Our spies were killed by them, my Lord
President,' a woman said.
'How dare you fail me!' he yelled, and with a flash
of his metal glove, he turned her to dust.

James Parker (11)
Mount St Mary's College, Spinkhill

99

House

One day a girl was sleeping. She got up and found that the door of the house was open. She heard some noises and she got scared. She saw blood on a piece of paper, it said, 'I'm in your house'. Then her mum yelled, 'Hello honey, I'm home!'

Ana Calinas (12)
Mount St Mary's College, Spinkhill

The Hunting Story

A man went out hunting in the woods with his
shotgun. When he got into the middle of the
woods he readied his shotgun. He shot because
he saw a rabbit and a cloud came off the ground.
Then a fox was laid dead instead of a big, wild
rabbit.

Dominic Walsham (11)
Mount St Mary's College, Spinkhill

Trapped

Bang! She walked down the old creaky stairs, trying to find where the noise came from. Unable to find anyone she ran to her butler's quarters, only to find him cold and white in a chair. She took his hand to wake him, but he couldn't be woken.

Jasmin Legdon (13)
Mount St Mary's College, Spinkhill

The Trenches

'In coming!' he shouted as bombs came crashing down. Bodies flying past and screams echoing through the trenches. Finally the bombing stopped and his best friend had been blown to pieces. As he picked up the dead man the large words 'Game Over' came onto the screen. 'Noooo!' I screamed.

Phill Brown (14)
Mount St Mary's College, Spinkhill

The Haunted Car

An old man slowly walked with a grim face
towards the door of the haunted car. As he
climbed into the car it started its engine and then
roared like a lion. Then the old man sat back. The
car took over the man's body, he was never seen
again.

Luke Whitehead (14)
Mount St Mary's College, Spinkhill

Surprise!

Isobel walked down the stairs, baseball bat in hand. Not knowing what was hiding in the dark, she flipped the light on. 'Surprise!' She shrieked with delight, stood in front of her was her boyfriend holding a puppy. 'Happy birthday!' She squeezed him tight, and they kissed passionately.

Bethany Forster (13)
Mount St Mary's College, Spinkhill

Fifty Words

Today our teacher told us that we would be writing something very exciting, but to our dismay it wasn't exciting. But I have to admit, it got me thinking. Our homework was to write it up neatly but I didn't know how to start it, so my mini saga begins.

Rhian Pearce (14)

Mount St Mary's College, Spinkhill

Who Was It?

Bang! We'd hit something. Something large. My dad slammed on the brakes and got out of the car slowly, to see what had happened. His face grew longer as he realised. Slowly walking, inch by inch, in the dark of the night. A body burnt and bruised, just lying there.

Isobel Unwin (14)

Mount St Mary's College, Spinkhill

Love Kills

As I stormed across the cliff edge, I received texts; 'I'm sorry, I love you. Forgive me.' I saw images of them in my head. My chest hurt. My eyes watery. My face was wet. I came to the cliff edge, I jumped, I regretted it. I loved him.

Frances Gray (12)
Mount St Mary's College, Spinkhill

Girl Snaps Her Leg Off

There was once a girl who was in a room when a zombie came in. Instead of him killing her, she snapped her legs and then chopped her head off, and then the zombie picked the head up and put it into the bin.

Cole Newell (11)

Mount St Mary's College, Spinkhill

109

The Fire

'Fire! Fire!' It's everywhere. Smoke consumes the science lab. Quickly and with no mercy, the fire destroys the building, only ash remains. Teachers are now furious, you can see the fire in their eyes. One of the children must have done this, but that's what teachers say.

Calum Lloyd (11)
Mount St Mary's College, Spinkhill

The Packrydon County Dream

One day I was asleep and had a dream. I landed
in a county called Packrydon. I saw some people
walking around the city. I walked up to them.
They were speaking in a different language. Then
I said, 'Where is McDonald's?' Then I woke up.

Riccardo Azzi (12)

Mount St Mary's College, Spinkhill

111

The Horrid Nightmare - The Will Walker Story

She walked into the cold, dark room, she closed the door. When she tried to turn on the light, it wasn't working. nothing was. Suddenly she heard footsteps in the kitchen, it was quiet again. She whispered, 'Hello?' Quickly there was a shout and a knife was stabbed into her.

William Walker (14)

Mount St Mary's College, Spinkhill

Shotgun Shock

I was walking home from the cinema. Me and John went to watch Barbie. It was quite scary, but oh well. I got home and found a granny breaking into my house. I tried to stop her, but it was too late. She shot me with a shotgun.

Will Jeonney (11)
Mount St Mary's College, Spinkhill

Deceive Oneself

A long time ago, a thief tried to steal a bell with beautiful decoration, but he made a lot of noise banging an axe on the metal. So he covered his ears up and couldn't hear. He thought nobody else could hear, but of course they could and caught him.

Maggie Tsui (12)

Mount St Mary's College, Spinkhill

Zimbabwe

In an old dark factory in the north of Zimbabwe the people were having a nap. The people wanted to get out of Zimbabwe! They left it until nightfall then they left! They got to the heavily armed border. By morning ten remained alive in a prison cell. *Bang!*

Alistair McInulty (13)
Mount St Mary's College, Spinkhill

The Bullies

Sarah walks down the street when she sees *the bullies.*
This group of boys are bullies. They smoke, drink and are very drugged up. They carry knives and are after her, so she starts to run. Nearly home, but out of breath, she is in ...

Charlie Dempsey (11)
Mount St Mary's College, Spinkhill

Cookies In The Cupboard

Once there was a boy who went to get the
cookies out the top cupboard. He was standing
on the table worktop. He suddenly slipped off
and landed on his head. He died. The cookies
were in the bottom cupboard.

Michael Wallace (12)

Mount St Mary's College, Spinkhill

117

One Shot Kill

It all started with the SAS calling an assassination.
It required one captain and the best sniper.
They were flown in. After taking out the guards,
unnoticed, they hit problems. There was a search
party looking for them. They gave them the slip.
After locating the target, they shot him.

James Struggles (12)

Mount St Mary's College, Spinkhill

Untitled

One time, far away, there was a boy. He was called Tom, he had a dog. They went for a walk on the hill and got chased by a dragon, but they got down safely.

Tom Peel (12)

Mount St Mary's College, Spinkhill

The Day Of Horror

A long time ago in Krapine a person got killed.
The neighbours heard her scream and then it
stopped. They looked into the window and saw
blood on the walls, and there she was, lying
without a head.
The next day her head was on a spike.

Luke Whyman (11)
Mount St Mary's College, Spinkhill

Forbidden Love

I loaded my gun and went into the building. There he stood, facing the wall on the other side of the room. I put my gun up and said, 'This is the SAS!' I remember that so well and now I am married to one of the Danny. From Viper.

Harriet White (14)

Mount St Mary's College, Spinkhill

121

Express Fear

She sat still, rigid and petrified. The gnarled wooden door vibrated with the noise from the other side, louder and louder until it rattled in its frame. Sudden silence cut through the air. Then stillness. The atmosphere cut by the knife. The 8.32 to Paddington was on time. For once.

Eleanor Greener (13)

Nottingham Girls' High School, Nottingham

Untitled

She dodged out of the doorway and hurried along
the cobbled street. Frosted air hung over her and
her steps echoed off the walls. The glimpse of
shadow made her heart stop. She turned again
and again. Still there. Dead end. She turned and
sighed with relief - a shadow, hers.

Zelekha Abid (15)
Nottingham Girls' High School, Nottingham

123

Clifftop

I stood at the edge. I couldn't. I couldn't jump, but I had to; there was no other way out. The waves broke and crashed into the base of the cliff. I closed my eyes, took a deep breath, and jumped. Slowly, I opened my eyes - paragliding wasn't that bad.

Jessica Walsh (14)

Nottingham Girls' High School, Nottingham

Look Twice

Daisy was walking to the supermarket to buy some apples. As she approached the man, an elderly lady was clutching her umbrella, she was about to cross the road whilst the lights were still green. I was staring at her. Then she fell. She hit the ground hard. Nothing moved.

Charlotte Foster (15)

Nottingham Girls' High School, Nottingham

The Umbrella

She clutched her umbrella tightly; it was the only possession she had left. 'Olivia.' Her heart hammered hard against her ribs. She turned around and saw him. Her knees locked, her feet rooted to the ground. He took aim and fired. *Crack!* She fell. The umbrella dropped and rolled away.

Zena Tansley Ahmed

Nottingham Girls' High School, Nottingham

The Best Memory

He wasn't that special, I suppose, but in the park
on that sunny day, with bees buzzing in the trees,
he seemed like the greatest thing in the world. I
didn't think he'd do it at first. But he did kiss me.
I was unbelievably ecstatic. Then his girlfriend
appeared.

Emma Scriver (14)
Nottingham Girls' High School, Nottingham

127

Terrorist

The phone sat in his pocket. Friends smiled as they passed by, he couldn't respond. Guilt rose in his throat, hard as rock. Checking the time and with fingers shaking, he dialled. A barely audible beeping sound began, counting down the seconds.

Two minutes later, the bomb exploded. *Bang! Bang!*

Lizzie Rudin (15)

Nottingham Girls' High School, Nottingham

The Forest

Alice could feel the hot breath crawling down her neck with heartbeat of footsteps behind. Step by step she drifted through the dark forest and listened for the paws crossing against the pebbles. As she approached the darkness, she waited for the pounce! The paws sunk and the mouth bit.

Lydia Bailey (15)
Nottingham Girls' High School, Nottingham

Bye-Bye Dorothy!

Dorothy went to the Grand Hotel to spend the night. By ten flights of stairs Dorothy was very tired. She decided to sit down on the dark brown carpet. Leaning against a mahogany clock, she regained her breath. Suddenly, with an almighty thud, Dorothy was flattened. Such shame.

Catherine Benson (14)
Nottingham Girls' High School, Nottingham

Mission

Sally was ready for her mission. Armed only with a cupcake and a torch, she took off. All of a sudden the shaking started, rocking, trembling, making her nervous, but she was brave. She opened the catch, but it was too late, the rocket swerved out of control, then crashed.

Hannah Clark (15)

Nottingham Girls' High School, Nottingham

Evil

My hands were trembling. The world passed by slowly. The knife felt cold in my hot, sweaty hands. He deserved it, he should be sorry. I hate him! He's pure evil. My heartbeat was the only sound I could hear. I plunged the knife into his chest. Deafening silence.

Jasmine Bavington (13)
Nottingham Girls' High School, Nottingham

Destiny

She was crouched in a shadowy corner, her limp
body curled in a ball. She lifted her eyelids and
her fiery eyes seared through brain. She seemed
weak, but she lifted me into the darkness. I didn't
want to go, but I had no choice.

Emily Dove (13)
Nottingham Girls' High School, Nottingham

133

The Graveyard

Derek yelped as he felt a sharp knife sink into his leg. It came from the shadows, eerie and silent. A tree rustled behind him. Derek knew this was the end. A silhouette appeared from the waters. The silhouette held up a knife, similar to the one in his leg.

Josey Robinson (13)
Nottingham Girls' High School, Nottingham

Human

The girl looked around the town, it was pitch-black and eerie. She suddenly saw the figure in the mist. It was a wolf, it lunged at its victim. The girl died painfully but very quickly. The wolf stood up, it shrank slowly and the fur disappeared. It was human.

Emma Still (13)
Nottingham Girls' High School, Nottingham

135

The Many Adventures Of Izzie And Harris

Harris pushed her way through the elongated towering trees. The animals hooted and howled as Izzie clumsily tripped over an overhanging branch. They braved on, wary of every noise and movement in the surrounding area. Suddenly a piercing scream yelped out. 'Cut!' the director cried and the scene was over.

Isobel Thompson (13)

Nottingham Girls' High School, Nottingham

Time Never Ends

The red chicken was running away. Away from the purple dragon. The smell of burning was in the air. The heavy thud of footsteps shook Magicland. The chicken was slow, the dragon was fast, it was getting closer. Closer! Closer! Then the world stood still. Everything stopped. Time stood still …

Olivia Hamilton (13)

Nottingham Girls' High School, Nottingham

Escape

Her wings fluttered gracefully. She swerved and swooped amongst the flowers. They were following. A tiny somersault amongst the moss, unseen by humans. She hid delicately, a sprig of grass securing her place. They sped on through the air. Her hair was ruffled. She was disturbed, but safe. For now.

Lottie Baxter (13)

Nottingham Girls' High School, Nottingham

The Near Miss!

As Jess and Alice soared through the clouds,
they heard a … *bang*. 'What was that?' said Jess,
curiously. 'It's quite close.' *Bang!* 'It's getting
closer.'
'Oh no, it's … it's, what is that?' screamed Alice.
As the giant creature was getting nearer, Alice and
Jess were more scared. *Phew*, they escaped.

Alice Richards (13)

Nottingham Girls' High School, Nottingham

139

That Day!

My heart was pounding. My head spinning. This was it, the real thing. As I stepped through the door, fifty eyes started to glare at me. I was so nervous. As I walked, each of my steps echoed through the dark, cold corridor. It was my first day at school.

Sophie Holmes (12)
Nottingham Girls' High School, Nottingham

Flamey The Dragon And The Evil Dragon Slayer

Once there was a dragon whose name was
Flamey. He was a seriously misunderstood
dragon.
One day a dragon slayer came to Flamey's cave
to kill him. Flamey tried to explain he was a good
dragon. Reluctantly Flamey breathed fire to keep
the slayer away. Then the slayer killed Flamey …

Zoë Nora Crowther (12)
Nottingham Girls' High School, Nottingham

A Warning Song

Her voice echoed against the cavern walls. She
sang like an angel, but her song was a warning.
Her long, sparkling tail seemed to dissolve and left
in its place were legs. Her head did the same and
her teeth were replaced by daggers and her eyes
turned blood-red …

Gabrielle Roper (13)

Nottingham Girls' High School, Nottingham

Silent, Alone ... Scared

'Stop!' A scream ripped through the silence of the dimly-lit street. There it lay, cold, bloody and stone-cold dead ... but what had happened, who had done this, and why? Only one boy knew - but where was he now? He was walking the New York streets, at dawn ... alone.

Daisy Nisbet (13)
Nottingham Girls' High School, Nottingham

143

Bullet, Bang, Blackout

A bullet whistled past, 2cm from his ear. His legs were lead, but he forced himself to stagger on. Then *bang!* Pain seared through his body and he felt as if his back was on fire. Blackness enveloped him …

Days later, a boy was found floating in the Thames … Dead.

June Ng (13)
Nottingham Girls' High School, Nottingham

The Thief

Run! He dodged. He ran. He looked back. Still there. Still following. He clutched the precious bundle to his chest. Being caught was not an option. He leapt over a pram and ducked under a young woman's handbag. Run! He had to run. A voice cried, 'You, stop! Stop thief!'

Katherine Hopewell (14)
Nottingham Girls' High School, Nottingham

The Unknown

Bang! Mary shot up from her bed, scanning her surroundings suddenly feeling alert. There was silence. Nothing had moved. She was safe. Mary relaxed slightly and slipped back under the duvet. She was just about to fall asleep when … *snap!* The little girl was snatched from her bed.

Brogan Shelby Jamson (14)
Nottingham Girls' High School, Nottingham

Under Pressure

I desperately tried to breathe but it was pointless - my air flow was being blocked by the squeezing sensation around my neck. My life was being brutally sucked away, along with my will to live. My lungs were screaming for the burning to stop. But it didn't; I was dying …

Tehillah Hinds (14)

Nottingham Girls' High School, Nottingham

The Invalid

Len and the family gathered round the hearthside; faces lit with flames and festivities. A grandchild put a cracker on his head. Valiant smiles sufficed. A fuse burnt out and somewhere in the house a real one did. Laughter followed darkness with the reluctance of dawn. 'Let the games begin.'

Lottie Limb (15)
Nottingham Girls' High School, Nottingham

Vertigo

Christopher Brown was inspired by the film 'New Moon' when Bella decided to go cliff jumping. He eagerly climbed to the top of the nearest cliff. However when he reached the top and peered cautiously over the edge, he remembered about his fear of heights. Slightly disappointed, he climbed down.

Abbie Flewitt (15)
Nottingham Girls' High School, Nottingham

Shatter And Scare!

My face suddenly shot a metre long, as the window smashed into a thousand tiny pieces. Was I having an hallucination or was it real? I saw a dark, mystical silhouette creeping into my room. I ran into my bed, covered my face. Something licked me. It was my cat.

Mia-Louise Adcock (12)

Nottingham Girls' High School, Nottingham

The Exit

Heart pounding in my ears, I gasped a last breath. Resisting my body being dragged up high, my eyelids flickered. Suddenly I plummeted down into a seemingly bottomless icy pool, spray whipping my cheeks, greeted by, 'Thank you for riding this log flume, please make your way to the exit.'

Mia Day (12)
Nottingham Girls' High School, Nottingham

Waiting ...

Time ticked slowly by, as the woman tried to control her quivering hands. *Tick-tock, tick-tock.* Sweat dribbled down her forehead. Her phone suddenly started to buzz loudly. Taking a deep breath, she answered the phone. 'Hello?'
'Hello, is this Sophie Jones speaking?'
'Yes, why?'
'You got the job!'

Hannah Burton (12)
Nottingham Girls' High School, Nottingham

Blood Pumping Excitement

I opened my eyes … A thick, scarlet liquid was smeared over the greasy floor. As I sat up, my stomach tightened, my head span, my eyes refocused on my worn and dirty jeans. They were stained with dried dirt. The enveloping and towering trees reminded me of the paintball fight.

Alice Williams (11)

Nottingham Girls' High School, Nottingham

153

Untitled

She woke up to a bang! The door blew open, creaking. There was a red, sticky substance on the floor and as she trod in it, she heard noises from the toilet. Screaming and shouting. She tiptoed through and pushed the door open to find … her sister with the ketchup.

Hannah Fielding (11)
Nottingham Girls' High School, Nottingham

The Shadow That Appeared At My Door

I was sweating like a pig. I could hardly move at all. My heart was beating so fast, my vision went fuzzy. The door started squeaking open. I could hear the wind howling around me. I switched my light on. A shadow appeared … Billy, my cat, strode through the door.

Philippa Mitchell (12)

Nottingham Girls' High School, Nottingham

155

Don't Do That In The Night

I woke up. My bed was thumping. The doors
were shaking, the wind was blowing. My windows
were rustling, my heart was beating. The floors
were creaking, footsteps were coming, getting
quieter and quieter. The door started to open. I
started shaking. 'Jemmima, you scared me! Don't
do that again!'

Zara Yasmin (11)

Nottingham Girls' High School, Nottingham

The Sound

A bead of sweat rolled down her face. Her big, brown eyes were fixed ahead. *Boom! Boom! Boom!* went the sound in her ears. She cowered back, afraid of what was in front of her face. *Click!* It was pitch-dark … The lights flicked on and the credits started rolling.

Sana Zaman (12)
Nottingham Girls' High School, Nottingham

An Earthquake?

The floor started to shake. Suddenly the whole world tilted sideways and before I knew it, I was being thrown against a metal wall. Three seconds later, I was tilted the other way! The world juddered to a halt. The door opened and I stepped off the fairground ride.

Ellie Swain (12)

Nottingham Girls' High School, Nottingham

Quick As A Cheetah

She darted down the path. Sweat on her head
and her face bright red. She quickly glanced
behind her and sped up even more to make her
almost as quick as a cheetah. She looked back
again and saw something red in the distance. The
Red Line bus had arrived.

Bethany Pownall (11)
Nottingham Girls' High School, Nottingham

The Taste Of Blood

Her tongue slid across her teeth, fresh blood, salty, lingering. She swallowed, wincing as the rusty tang hit the back of her throat. Stumbling to the sink she filled a glass with a jet of water and knocked it back. Milk teeth were such a pain when they fell out!

Christie Kyriacou (13)
Nottingham Girls' High School, Nottingham

Faster And Faster

It's coming closer and closer, straight in my direction. My heart is pounding, I can barely breathe, it's bouncing out my chest. It's coming faster and faster, closer and closer, louder and louder, second by second. I put my arms out with fright and amazingly, I catch the cricket ball!

Amelia Widdowson (11)

Nottingham Girls' High School, Nottingham

161

Untitled

Where is she? I can't see her, she's not here or over there. The traffic is going past too fast for me to see her, if she's there. I can see her car and flat, but not her. She couldn't have taken the bus, she wouldn't have, she hates buses.

Yosha Puri (12)

Nottingham Girls' High School, Nottingham

The Rattling Closet

I spun around! I was certain something was there.
I grabbed hold of the leg of the chair. The closet
rattled, I kicked it down furiously. I viciously
whacked the interior of the wardrobe. Hesitantly
I checked who I'd beaten, I removed the cloth.
Thankfully it was only Uncle Minty!

Kiran Nijran (12)
Nottingham Girls' High School, Nottingham

It's Gone

I stood in front of my old school. Suddenly the ground started shaking. It looked like the ground had just broken. It felt like the world was coming to an end. Finally the demolition finished and it was just a heap of ash on the ground. It was over.

Bethan Manktelow (12)

Nottingham Girls' High School, Nottingham

Where's My Dad?

I am absolutely terrified! He was going to be gone
for 20 minutes, it's been more than an hour. I
don't know what to do, I'm alone. What should I
do? Call the police? Go and look for him? 'Boo!'
He was behind me, wearing an alien costume.
How weird!

Hope Kightley (12)
Nottingham Girls' High School, Nottingham

Game Over

We were driving along Woodview Road. Diana, the lollipop lady, waved us over the crossing. Supermarkets, newsagents and boutiques flashed past us. Then suddenly everything was gone. Like a blank screen it was. We had crashed into a van ... I couldn't believe it, I looked at the screen ...
Game Over.

Anya Barnes (12)

Nottingham Girls' High School, Nottingham

Mortal Death

The man struck down. Her heart was pierced,
but she was unharmed. Bloodstained blonde hair,
her eyes became deep blue in rage. She shook
the man off her and she threw herself into him. It
was then he realised who she was - becoming a
mortal, death hadn't been easy.

Kylan Finch (13)

Nottingham Girls' High School, Nottingham

Right Or Wrong?

Rachel liked James, James liked Suzie. She knew this but hated Suzie for it. Once she got so angry she tried to get rid of Suzie … She told her that her parents were waiting for her in the park, so she could talk to James, but they weren't … he was …

Chloé Richardson (13)
Nottingham Girls' High School, Nottingham

Hide-And-Seek

Just then, Daisy heard a noise. She walked through the house trying to figure out what it could be. She entered her sister's bedroom. She saw the reflection in the mirror. The hairs on her back stood up. The reflection showed a man standing right behind her. She stood. Paralysed.

Mahdea Mughal (13)
Nottingham Girls' High School, Nottingham

Fate

Faster and faster. As I ran through the city, I felt nauseous, sick and dizzy. Why did it happen to me? Why me? I had to escape the clutches of the shadows. Turning a corner, I found myself in a dark alleyway. My heart was pounding, my fate awaited me …

Alice Malbon (13)
Nottingham Girls' High School, Nottingham

The Quicksand

The pregnant woman was stuck in the quicksand.
She had been pushed in by her furious partner,
angry in his fit. He had these fits and you couldn't
predict when he'd have one. It was too late; her
head was under the quicksand. Dead, along with
the baby! *Both dead!*

Georgia Frater-Wharmby (12)
Nottingham Girls' High School, Nottingham

A Thousand Times

Yandi slammed the cupboard door. She turned
away; it started shaking again. She twisted around
to face it. She had done it a thousand times, but
she was scared. Her hand shook as she grasped
the handle; she opened it, the door swung open,
but she didn't search the shadows …

Catherine Jones (13)
Nottingham Girls' High School, Nottingham

The Flames

The glass shattered. A shadow darted swiftly through the flickering lights, trying to escape fate. It shouldn't have been like this: he wasn't supposed to be the one to lose his life today. No, it was supposed to be the girl with fair hair - a dagger through her cruel heart.

Katerina Senior (13)
Nottingham Girls' High School, Nottingham

Thief!

I crept towards the classroom, as silent as a ghost. All I had in mind was to accomplish the mission. There he was! He reached towards the lunch boxes, stuffing himself with chocolate bars. I smiled to myself, *got him!* I crept closer. Then I jumped out and screamed, 'Thief!'

Natalie Tseu (13)

Nottingham Girls' High School, Nottingham

Abandoned

The water was at hip height now. I grabbed
the sail to stop myself from plummeting down
through the depths of the ocean. *This is the day,
the day I die. All alone.* My hands were getting
sweaty. They couldn't hold on anymore. I let go. I
lost all hope.

Beccy Ballantine (12)
Nottingham Girls' High School, Nottingham

Regret

He is going for his usual outing. This is just getting better and better. He is moving towards the forest; my favourite place as well. And that clingy, nervous nanny has left; how convenient - she let him play with matches! The blood's coming out now, but it's the wrong boy.

Sarah Quraishi (12)

Nottingham Girls' High School, Nottingham

Revenge

Pablo Berel stepped out of the Hotel Grande lobby, and on to the stained New York pavement; fluorescent logos and signs gleamed. The dirty-rich owner, Antonio Torres Claret Renaldi had to pay for what he'd done. He heard a scream. Heat scorched his neck; the raging inferno was alive.

Natasha Thomas (13)
Nottingham Girls' High School, Nottingham

The Empty Passage

The warmth of the wax tickles her arm. The candlestick shakes with every step. To explore an empty hotel means a secret unlocked. The dusty floorboards groan beneath each step through the deserted passage. Finally she arrives at the forbidden door - just one push to a new mystery.

Amelia Martin-Jones (13)
Nottingham Girls' High School, Nottingham

Gone

Gone. Dead, was he, who was loved by so many.
Why? Why was it him who had to go? So sudden.
So fast. One truck. One man. That's all it took for
one life to be stolen by the clutches of death. A
bang. A crash. Tears. Lights. Sirens. Gone.

Grace Hardy (12)
Nottingham Girls' High School, Nottingham

Snow White's Twist

Prince Charming leaned in to kiss her, the dwarves whispered to each other, querying if it would work. Prince kissed her. He waited then frowned. She didn't wake up. Suddenly a dwarf screamed as a fat ogre came near the house. He saw her. She awoke before he did anything …

Elizabeth Barnett (12)

Nottingham Girls' High School, Nottingham

Why?

'Why?' said Billy, 'do we always have honey?'
'All you do is complain!' said Betty. Roaring wheels
above made the roof crumble.
'Urgh, that's why this place was cheap,' moaned
Dad.
'C'mon, let's go out!' laughed Mum.
The badger family came out of their set and into
the world above.

Anna Jootun (11)
Nottingham Girls' High School, Nottingham

181

In The Woodlands

The fairy lives outside the window, under the
leafy, jade moss. She has feeble features, silky hair
and doll-like feet that patter through the trees.
She runs along, without a fear, through the wood
full of mythical creatures. She hops, skips and
jumps, right into a leprechaun …

Grace Walters (12)

Nottingham Girls' High School, Nottingham

Bored

Goldilocks was bored. School was boring.
She was up to her ears in boredom because
something was always happening at Ex-Fairy Tale
High. Like the day the wicked witch showed up,
or when Captain Hook came after Peter Pan.
Goldilocks was normal, but she never met the
bears.

Emily Stuart (12)
Nottingham Girls' High School, Nottingham

183

Ending Life

I'm Gluto Moniplot and come from the planet
Zortog. We're at war with our neighbour planet,
Potis. I've always wished that it would end, that
it'd all stop! That way I wouldn't be lying on my
deathbed, with the love of my life, Shelly. My
body dies, I survive.

Kajal Tamber (12)
Nottingham Girls' High School, Nottingham

Kindness?

Stars fell at night. The moon shone at its brightest. The little owl hobbled out of its dome-like nest. His eyes twinkling like crystals in the midnight sky. He stared at the dew, glistening on the grass below. A small, brown mouse scuttled by, but he let it go.

Bhuvana Sudarshan (11)
Nottingham Girls' High School, Nottingham

185

Untitled

Just one jump, that's all it took to ruin her career. Just one leap. A leap of faith. You could taste the fear. She tried to triple-barrel jump, the oldest trick in the book. Just that sound, a quick wrong landing, she was paralysed for life.

Georgia Sail (12)
Nottingham Girls' High School, Nottingham

Hello

Coming back from dance was a girl, she was all dressed up in her dancing clothes. The girl stopped to find a sign on her house saying 'Grime Investigation'. *It must be Kim and Aggie,* she thought. She entered the house. 'Hello,' said a strange voice. The voice echoed …

Sophia Kapur (11)
Nottingham Girls' High School, Nottingham

That Dream

She pulled out the knife, leaning towards her
friend. 'What are you doing?'
'Getting ready to kill my dad!'
'Don't, he's done so much for you.'
'All he's done for me has made my life horrible.'
I woke, why was I going to do this to the father I
love?

Georgia Hawkins (12)
Nottingham Girls' High School, Nottingham

Beautiful

I glare at Maisy's beauty, her features so delicately
divine. Her crimson hair sways gently in the wind.
She always wears the most beautiful fragrance.
Though her siblings are hideous, she's back-
stabbingly angelic and always gets all the guys.
This is because Maisy's a rose and I'm a thistle.

Sarah Robson (12)
Nottingham Girls' High School, Nottingham

Books Ablaze

Walking through the forest, I smelt burning. A horrid, choking odour. Running towards the source, the whiff of petrol appeared, so strong, I could hardly breathe. Standing next to the roaring fire, I inhaled a suffocating scent of words being engulfed by a hungry flame. Sitting, I smelt books ablaze.

Julia Auer (12)

Nottingham Girls' High School, Nottingham

What I Live For!

My feet lingered on the edge of the cliff, my eyes watering from the sharp gust of wind. For a brief moment my nerves overpowered the thrill, but this was what I lived for. Cliff-diving.

Saskia Peach (13)
Nottingham Girls' High School, Nottingham

191

The Dream That Came True

My heart was pounding, as my first fashion
collection walked onto the runway. My idol,
Christopher Gabarina, was sitting in the audience.
As my collection was coming to an end, someone
tapped me on the shoulder, it was Christopher.
He loved my collection and bought it for £10,000.

Joanna Huang (12)

Nottingham Girls' High School, Nottingham

The Magic Garbage Tip

The garbage tip. Dirty, smelly, disgusting. There I
was, standing right next to it. Rotting apple cores,
crunched up paper, oozing with goo, cups of
lumpy, mouldy, thick milk. It was gross, so gross it
made me cringe. My stomach churned, my head
spun, I felt sick. Then I fell.

Estée Coulthard-Boardman (12)
Nottingham Girls' High School, Nottingham

Silent Storm

The raging sea glistened in the light of the moon. It smashed against the sides of the ship. The storm approached silently. Everyone held things down and hoped that the sea wouldn't get any rougher, but it did. Suddenly there was a cry. 'I can see the harbour lights … !'

Yusra Abdelhamid (12)
Nottingham Girls' High School, Nottingham

Doggy Day Care

One day Lazy Luke was running along the
pavement, when suddenly Jumping Jack was
running along the same pavement. They both
met and stopped outside a gate which they both
turned into. They went inside the house. They
looked around and went wild! They'd arrived at
their doggy day care.

Emma Hinchley (13)
Nottingham Girls' High School, Nottingham

The Fight

This pearly white creature plunged forward,
the battle had begun! I grabbed the shiny, sharp
sword and bravely leapt forward and attacked
the courageous beast. I had surprisingly missed.
Determined to not miss this time, avoiding
everything this monster gave me, I tried again,
disappointed as he got there first.

Azeema Iqbal (12)

Nottingham Girls' High School, Nottingham

No Escape

His heart quickened. There wasn't a way out. No escape. They were going to get him, whatever he did. Suddenly, a midnight-black Ferrari sped around the corner. Stranded. 'We know it was you, you have to face the punishment.'
'No I swear …' *Bang!*
Falling to the floor, he gasped.

Hannah Garvey (13)
Nottingham Girls' High School, Nottingham

197

The Diver

It was watching her. Watching as the diver swam around the wreck, taking pictures and disturbing the wildlife. She was being careless. It decided someone … or something, should teach her a lesson. It waited for her to swim inside the wreck - then followed her. She turned around, saw it, screamed.

Charlotte Jones (12)

Nottingham Girls' High School, Nottingham

The Creep!

She ran away, hoping no one would find her.
Slowly someone crept up to her. *Roar!* Smeared
blood was everywhere. *How disgusting,* she
thought! Her life was in great danger. *What to do?*
The growling voice grew louder and louder - all
wooden doors locked and shut with no
way out …

Iram Khan (13)

Nottingham Girls' High School, Nottingham

199

Untitled

Standing there, gazing down at my feet to see
old, worn-out boots, with my swollen feet inside
them. Standing on nothing but dry, dusty ground,
locked in like an animal. Kicking the stones out of
the way, my stinging eyes wandered over to the
prisoners, hearing their deafening screams.

Sophie Williams (13)
Nottingham Girls' High School, Nottingham

Unnecessary Love!

I rotated my head for a glance at what stood
behind me. He began to creep towards me. My
head drooped towards the floor. In front of me
he stood. I glared into his blue eyes. His hand fell
into mine. He gently stroked my cheek. His lips
covered mine …

Jessica Spencer (12)
Nottingham Girls' High School, Nottingham

Ten Seconds To Midnight

The clock was ticking, it was ten seconds to midnight. She was hiding round the corner, ready to pounce! Nobody was expecting it to happen. Everybody was running. Time was running out. She was getting closer and closer and closer. Everyone's heart was pounding so hard, and then it happened …

Claudia Billings (12)

Nottingham Girls' High School, Nottingham

Alone And Afraid

I heard the knock at 10.00. The door creaked
open slowly and a tall, thin shadow appeared.
'Dad?' I whispered. No reply. A figure carrying
a trident with my parents' heads on two of the
spokes came in, my brother's on the remaining.
'No room for you,' he said.

Danielle Ball (12)
Nottingham Girls' High School, Nottingham

The Midnight Hunter

It swooped, soared, towered. Below it the silent moor was silver in the moonlight. Suddenly a rustle and … *snatch!* An unsuspecting mouse flew to its death, the creature's hunting complete.

Alexandra Lodge (13)

Nottingham Girls' High School, Nottingham

The Fallen Angel

Darkness; it was all around. The cold, damp
lack of light clung to everything. The girl turned,
her dress hung limp and transparent, flapping
uselessly around her legs, they were bare.
Maggots crawled up that slender form from the
earthy floor, to her black feathered wings: once
beautiful, now rotten.

Morgan Metheringham (13)
Nottingham Girls' High School, Nottingham

205

Split Decision

Anger surged through my veins, my pulse quickened. In that moment I knew what I had to do. The dagger I held in my sweaty hand suddenly seemed to weigh ten times more. I had to kill her … or did I? I realised I was possessed - I was mad.

Frances Benson (13)
Nottingham Girls' High School, Nottingham

Carnivorous Creatures

Commonly misconceived as a cruel carnivorous
crustacean. Spending its days submerged beneath
the surface, concealed in coral and crevices.
Swimming to the seabed, whilst other fish sleep,
it prowls, clicks its claws and camouflages.
Deafening *splash!* Strange creature, twist, turn,
net enclosing, slowly suffocating, hit on head.
Lobster bisque.

Susannah McMillan (13)

Nottingham Girls' High School, Nottingham

Chilli

Sweat poured down my face as I sat, my whole body cold as ice as things started to blur. Scanning the room, I couldn't tell what anything was anymore. In the distance I saw a white light, the floor swayed up to me. Why did I eat that chilli?

Alicia Fitzgerald (13)
Nottingham Girls' High School, Nottingham

The Trick

Panting, I burst into the room. I could hear footsteps behind me. Then, I caught a glimpse of the key. I reached out for it. I could almost feel the glisten. I closed my shaking hand around it, only for it to dissolve before my eyes. I had been tricked.

Emma Stewart (13)

Nottingham Girls' High School, Nottingham

209

Colours

A blue sun? Pink grass? Orange leaves? Where am I? I remember, I was looking at the picture. I must have fallen in. Green carrots, delicious! Purple bananas, yummy! But there is a voice behind, dragging me out the picture. Then … 'What are your impressions of our coloured contact lenses?'

Meggie Jordan (12)

Nottingham Girls' High School, Nottingham

What Is It?

'There … did you see it?'
'No, what?'
'Look, there it is again! But I can't quite make it
out … can you?'
'No … it sort of looks like a tall, slim figure,
creeping …'
'Yes, it definitely looks mysterious, creeping, low
to the ground … slowly, silently … yes … and it's
coming this way!'

Lydia Green (13)
Nottingham Girls' High School, Nottingham

Monarch Of The Sky

In the air, the mighty warrior dives, twisting, twirling, soaring, swirling. Its prey, a mere dove, flees for its life, but in vain. The imperial bird is too fast; it streaks ahead and snaps up the lesser avian. Nature's cycle has taken its course and the eagle is proven glorious.

Mathilda Pynegar (13)
Nottingham Girls' High School, Nottingham

Race For Survival

Massive, heavy leaf. Crushing. Must reach nest before sky darkens. Branches all around, making an assault course. Heavy, crushing. Another step forward. *Crash!* My friend, flattened by rain globe. Nothing I can do. Must keep moving. *Splash!* Dodging my way through. Faster and faster! Nearly there. Closer, closer. But … *splat!*

Prishita Maheshwari (13)
Nottingham Girls' High School, Nottingham

213

Lost And Found

Lost, seeking help, nowhere to go. Wandering on your own through a deserted forest. *Snap!* Phew, it's just a branch! Trembling, you hear noises, who is it? Or what is it? Turning around you see nothing, but someone's breathing down your neck. Your heartbeat increases, you turn around and …

Georgiana Zowonu (12)
Nottingham Girls' High School, Nottingham

The Runaway

Always running, trying to escape, venturing out to someplace new. Wondering where to go next and needing to get as far away as possible. Running, running, running. I can't stop running. Needing to start a new life, away from here. I can't turn back now, I can never return now.

Siân McIntyre (12)

Nottingham Girls' High School, Nottingham

The Girl, The Dog And The Cynophobia

She was running … she didn't really know what
she was running from, but what she did know
scared her. The creature was small but deadly. It
had fangs (well, most probably anyway) and sharp
claws. Also, the creature answered to the name
of Cuddles, the white toy poodle,
demon puppy …

Sophie Rees (13)
Nottingham Girls' High School, Nottingham

As I Write

As I sit here, writing this saga, chaos surrounds me. People fighting, knives slashing, guns firing, people collapsing in agony. The hooded men peel off their balaclavas. I, in the safety of my home, see that their faces are not those of humans. Black, bottomless eyes, twisted, insane mouths. Tortured.

Vicky Filor (13)
Nottingham Girls' High School, Nottingham

Flying High Above The Clouds

Flying high above the clouds which fill the moonlit
skies, the singing birds swoop down through the
forests! When suddenly a wolf appears, growling,
stomach empty. It pounces on the flying flock,
who fly back up, higher, higher, further into the
milky night sky and behind the glowing moon!

Sophie Louise Corah (13)
Nottingham Girls' High School, Nottingham

The Shadow

I slowly, silently crept through the trees, feeling my way through the darkness. *Crack!* A twig snapped behind me, jolting me, alerting me. I blindly spun around, feeling unsafe. Nothing. Silence. I carried on, faster, cautiously creeping through the forest. Suddenly a shadow engulfed me from the darkness. Alone. Trapped.

Tizzy Gill (12)
Nottingham Girls' High School, Nottingham

A Close Encounter With The Ocean Floor

As we sailed along on a calm, sunny day I spotted something in the waves. *What's that?* I wondered. I leaned closer, but the boat started to tip. It was too late, I was three feet underwater and sinking fast. The next thing I saw was the ocean floor.

Freya Corner (13)

Nottingham Girls' High School, Nottingham

The Shadow

The horrifying taboo converges all of your thoughts. It jumps with precise movement, doesn't give you a chance! You run with relentless effort, sweat cascading down your face. 'Look out,' you hear someone bellow but their screams are muffled. You pump your legs harder. The shadow is approaching you.

Panashe Mabeza (12)
Nottingham Girls' High School, Nottingham

221

The Performance

Crash! Then the lights went out. 'What is happening? I can't see anything. Where am I? More importantly, who am I? Oh my goodness, what do I do now?'

Lights go on. 'That was just two words - absolutely amazing! Bravo! Definitely one of the best performances. You're in the show!'

Preeni Shah (13)
Nottingham Girls' High School, Nottingham

Lost

The icy wind whipped my face. I didn't know
where I was or where I was going. Suddenly a
large silhouette appeared through the dense
fog and snow. My first thought was that the
abominable snowman would eat me. Closer and
closer it came … 'Thank God we found you!'

Claire Norris (13)
The Minster School, Southwell

Haunted Nightmares

In the dark, the hunter lurked. The prey had arrived. The temple was quiet. The hunter stalked his victim. The prey ran, faster, faster, *thud!* The hunter jumped down in front of him.
'Why me?' cried the prey.
The reply was, 'For the motherland.' The blade went into the prey.

Alex Wright (13)
The Minster School, Southwell

Untitled

The car crashed through the solid brick wall. The windows smashed and bodywork crumpled. The driver died and his red blood splashed on the white leather seats.

Shakeal Fraser (12)

The Minster School, Southwell

Freedom

I felt the sun beating on my back and eyes watching me. The guard drew back his arm, then suddenly there was a stinging in my back. The pain was overpowering. My knees buckled, I was on the ground. I lay for hours. Night fell, I ran … freedom was mine!

Megan Flintham (13)

The Minster School, Southwell

Running For Keeps

I was lost, alone forever. I was running for my life as my worst predator was trying to take it from me. I thought it was all over … but it wasn't. I saw a safe place and ran as fast as I could. I was safe - for now anyway.

Jenny Hurst (13)
The Minster School, Southwell

A Rude Awakening

It came closer and closer, until I could feel it staring right at me. The smell of rotting fish and blood emanating from its claw-filled mouth. A rouge ribbon emerged from nowhere and felt rough against my cheek. He smugly plodded off, for he had victoriously woken me up.

Zak Dibben (13)

The Minster School, Southwell

The Assassin

On top of a building; balancing. An unknown king of this city, surveys life below like a hungry hawk. Someone down there knows what happened. He needs to know. Gunfire. He stands up and jumps, diving, the wind on his face. He takes out the villain.

Jackson Brooksby (13)

The Minster School, Southwell

229

The Pier

The pier was still, the moonlight shone down on it like a spotlight. The area was quiet as I dipped my feet into the cold, blue water. I was alone in the darkness of the gloomy night. A flash of yellow darted under my feet. I saw its teeth. Blackness.

Emma Branston (13)

The Minster School, Southwell

Frogs Or Not?

Princess Tamsin danced through Fairy Glen,
looking for frogs to kiss. Aha! A frog! She kissed
it quickly. Nothing happened. Ah well, she didn't
want to get married anyway. Disappointed log
princes looked at the hidden witch.
'You didn't think I'd make it that easy?' she
chuckled.

Evie Hoggard (13)
The Minster School, Southwell

231

Gold Lava

As I walked through the forest, I slipped and fell
down a hole, a deep, dark hole. As I awoke I
saw a tunnel. I went along the tunnel and I saw
a kingdom of pure gold, but the only way across
was to cross the bridge across the lava!

Ryan Hazard (12)
The Minster School, Southwell

Bang! Bang! Bang!

Bang! Bang! Bang! Bang! I was on my Xbox and the screen went white! A voice said, 'I've got your aerial.' I was terrified! I rushed downstairs, told my mum.
She laughed, 'It's the electrician, he's changing the aerial!' We laughed for hours upon end.

Domm Stockbridge (13)
The Minster School, Southwell

233

Holiday Surprise

I woke up to another day on Mystical Moor. The
musty smell of it greeting me again. It was then
that I realised I was nowhere near my camp.
Strange, inhuman faces stared back at me. They
were dancing round me, chanting. It got faster
then … 'Happy April Fool's Day!'

Radhika Orozco (13)

The Minster School, Southwell

Terror Café

I walked into the dark, murky room. A tall, bald man slowly trudged up to me and asked if I wanted a drink. 'Please, could I have a hot chocolate?' I mumbled. The barmaid came up with teeth in the wrong place and a wart. This was a terror café!

James Pritchett (11)
The Minster School, Southwell

235

It Is All My Fault

I heard shouting, every day of every week. I knew
what was coming. Something was wrong. Crying
was echoing throughout the house. Then my dad
left the house. Sadness was drawn onto my face. I
knew it was my fault. There was not a sound, the
house went completely silent.

Emily Durbin (12)
The Minster School, Southwell

Alone

'I miss you, Pete,' she whispered. The rain crashed, lashed and pounded down against the window. The wind whistled a sad tune through a hole in the wall, like the one in her heart, a part of her that had gone with her husband to the grave. 'I miss you.'

Daniel Jackson (12)
The Minster School, Southwell

Trapped

Trapped in a deep, dark hole. I heard a rustling.
A figure appeared. I sprinted towards what
appeared to be an opened door. Stranger still, it
led out of a rabbit hole. Looking back, the figure
was close. Suddenly, without warning, I opened
my eyes. It was all a dream!

Emily Hall (12)
The Minster School, Southwell

Star Wars

'We meet again,' said a dark shadow, then the room filled with light. 'You must die,' said the man who'd just shown his old, wrinkly face.

'No, I won't,' said the young Jedi, who brought his lightsaber out of his pocket, full of anger. 'Let's fight!'

Joshua Slack (12)
The Minster School, Southwell

239

Fairy Glen

We were in the high tops of the Scottish hills,
it was bright and sunny. There was a rumble,
the fairies flew away, the giants were coming. It
stopped, the fairies flew back down. It was really
gloomy. They had to defeat the giants, to be
happy forever and ever!

Jenni Fifoot (13)
The Minster School, Southwell

The Polar Fairy

Once upon a time there was a fairy kingdom.
All the fairies were the same, kind and helpful,
except for one who had the face of a bear. One
night the polar fairy ran away to a cave and two
days later returned with a magnificent face and
became queen.

Lauren Berry (13)
The Minster School, Southwell

Boom!

I could hear them from miles away. *Boom! Boom! Boom!* I broke into a run. I thought I was going to get away, but then I ran into one. Its face looked distorted. I could smell burning, but the worst thing was, I couldn't hear anything. Then I awoke.

Tom Winning

The Minster School, Southwell

Pixie Path

Pete the Pixie was flying around Pixie Path when he noticed something shiny on the floor. He flew down and realised that it was a human's coin! He went to a human shop and bought an ice cream. He went back and shared it with the others on Pixie Path!

Eve Whitehead (12)

The Minster School, Southwell

243

It Stared ...

It stared. With its long beard, it stared. I needed to get over. We needed to get over. Shivering in our hooves. It stared. We got halfway. He leapt in front of us, he tried to defeat us, his plan backfired. Never seen him again.

Millie Pargeter (12)
The Minster School, Southwell

I'm A Giant

I woke up tiredly but suddenly awakened when
I noticed I was not in my own bed. Frantically
I looked around. What was I doing here? I was
amazed by what I was seeing, but my biggest
question was, why was everyone so small?

Tilly Rayner (13)
The Minster School, Southwell

245

Mysterious Monday

Let me backtrack. I drowsily woke up at 7.45,
late as always. I opened my wardrobe - I was
sucked in. I then landed heavily back in my room,
but where was the laptop? I sneezed, boy was
it dusty. Where was I? Not 2010, of that I was
certain.

Lucy Menhennet (13)
The Minster School, Southwell

Polly The Pixie

As pixie Polly set off on her walk, she noticed a pretty pixie cave. With anticipation she stepped inside … she saw a fat fairy eating all the pretty pixie food. *That's a mean fairy.* Then she saw the yummy, scrummy chocolate ice cream. *Yum,* she thought and joined in!

Shannon Wilson (12)

The Minster School, Southwell

247

A Story Of Sid

Once there was a boy called Sid, who ran into a tree. When Sid hit the tree he turned into a tree and the tree turned into him. The tree, called Harold, just stood there. Harold found out he could walk and ran back into the tree.

Isaac Richmond (13) & Leo Lam

The Minster School, Southwell

It ...

He ran, slipping on the wet pavestones. It followed. It didn't have a name or species, but it followed. Chasing the man through streets, parks and back alleys, until they got to a dead end. The end of him ...

Ashley Warwick (12)
The Minster School, Southwell

The Three Little Pigs

The three little pigs were at their mother's house.
They all moved out. One little pig made a house
out of straw. One of the pigs made a house out of
sticks and one made a house of bricks. The wolf
blew the houses made of straw and sticks down.

Craig Westerman (11)
The Minster School, Southwell

Deadland

People screaming in despair. Zombies roaming
the streets, terrorising citizens. A person's
screams echo through the streets. It suddenly
stops. *Crack! Munch!* This unsuspecting citizen's
life has been cut short. Who will ever know what
will happen to this scenario?

Laurence Bradford (12)
The Minster School, Southwell

251

Ben & Jerry's Ice Cream

Ben and Jerry are best friends.
One day Ben goes missing and Jerry finds him
in the chocolate factory with Charlie and Willie
Wonka. He teaches them how to make ice cream
and now they're famous and are loved by many.
That is why we have Ben and Jerry's today.

Betsy Sweeney (11)
The Minster School, Southwell

The Haunted House

As she got closer to the deserted house, it became clear the rumours were true. The smashed windows and rotting door that hung wide open. It was blatant nobody had lived there in decades. It suddenly all fit. Although she'd had her doubts before, the house was clearly haunted.

Clara Best (14)

The Minster School, Southwell

253

A Demon's Choice

The destruction of a hero satisfied evil, but not this evil. This creature wanted to watch the world burn while its inhabitants begged for mercy or death, but one demon turned against his brothers to defend Earth. 'Traitor, your death will please my masters,' yelled Mirrobog.

Samuel Downing (14)
The Minster School, Southwell

Collisions

The smashed car headlights flickered as Charlotte was wheeled into the pristine ambulance and the paramedic attempted to stem the blood flow. Her mother squeezed her hand as the tiny beeps on her heart monitor faltered. A cold feeling crept over Charlotte. She smiled. It was finally over.

Jack Coupland (14)

The Minster School, Southwell

255

Love-Struck

Suddenly a piercing pain struck; a cry ripped through the air. I didn't need to be near her to realise he'd left. I knew he would, I told her he would, but she wouldn't believe me. The worst thing was that I couldn't stop him from hurting her.

Emily Wells (14)

The Minster School, Southwell

Why Me?

I could feel my face going red as the whole room
looked at me. I did not do that. My best friend
had told me to press a button, up on a stand in
the middle of the room. So I did! It made the
loudest noise ever. Why me?

Annie Beckett (14)

The Minster School, Southwell

Untitled

In a small village called Glenville, a boy called
Huntelaar climbed the great mountain and
entered the dragon's lair. It was dark and gloomy.
He had reached the furthest point. There it was,
the ring of the Niberlungen. He was about to take
it; the fire held him back.

Greg Salt (13)
The Minster School, Southwell

A Romantic Wonder

Henry's sixth wife asked him, 'Oh Henry, why did you kill all those innocent women? What had they done to you?'
'Well, let me tell you something, deary, I'll never kill you because our love is pure and forever.'
Katherine said, 'And I will you, my love, I will you.'

Joshua Vickers (13)
The Minster School, Southwell

259

Star Riders

The USS Star Rider came under fire. The crew
was shaken when a laser torpedo hit the side. 'All
shields are weak,' one crewman panicked.
Another announced, 'The EMP Cannon has been
charged Captain!'
The captain thought for a minute and ordered,
'Fire it.' The cannon fired.
'Finally safe!'

Conor Hind (13)

The Minster School, Southwell

The Car Crash

One day I was in a car with my friends. We were on the motorway going to the airport, when a car overtook us. We thought the driver was drunk. Then he braked and we drove into the back of him and crashed!

Luke Polak

The Minster School, Southwell

Born To Run

Darkness - where is my owner, where am I? It happened so fast, I got tricked into this van. Soon I will be a race dog for this man - a dog killer. The van is opening, a girl stands there crying. Her eyes are telling me to run away.

Natalie Abbott (12)

The Minster School, Southwell

Captured

Frog was sitting, nervously staring in every direction. Scared, worried, frightened. He had never seen underwater. He didn't want to be captured. He was young. He had never heard of birds. *Caww! Caww!* It swooped. Captured in vicious claws, Frog was being taken away. Frog was gone!

Bethany Gratton (12)

The Minster School, Southwell

Darkness

There wasn't even the sound of a clock, it was pitch-black. There were some behind me, they were creeping round too much for my liking. I began to run, they did, then it hit me like a rock dropping in water. After that, it was a blur.

Elliot Fairburn (11)

The Minster School, Southwell

Trapped!

I stood there, staring at the glistening rocks.
I could hear something. A split-second later,
water gushed towards me. I had to escape. I
swam strongly against the currant, I could see an
exit. I swam towards it and struggled out. The
shimmering sun shone on me. Freedom!

Georgina Clark (11)
The Minster School, Southwell

Bang!

Bang! All I could see was white. My head was spinning. I couldn't feel the pain, the adrenaline was flowing through my veins. Blood was running down my face: I felt my phone vibrate. I tried to stand up but my leg was broken. To live or to die … ?

Matthew Payton (13)
The Minster School, Southwell

The Battle

Joan could feel the horse under her, she could tell he was nervous. But what she was seeing, was even worse. She saw her men being terrified. They didn't want to die in battle. At this moment she was getting nervous. She sensed something was wrong, it wouldn't help her.

Samantha Plummer (14)

The Minster School, Southwell

Untitled

He's at home, on his own, parents are out. He
sits at the TV watching cartoons. The door
creaks. The boy jumps. He thinks it's his parents
with their shopping, then he realises it's the
chainsaw maniac, seeking revenge for something
the boy has not done. What next?

James Smith (13)

The Minster School, Southwell

The Kill

The polar bear walked on, starved and chilled by the bitter frost. Its eyes lit up as it sighted a hole in the ice. A seal came to breathe. He stood, ready to pounce, looking at his reflection shimmering around the hole. *Swoosh!* The bear was victorious!

Joel Rollitt (13)

The Minster School, Southwell

13 Friday Street

I walked on the path just after school finished. I was opening the front door and heard moaning in the house. I felt so scared, I was sweating from panic. I opened the door and found horrid creatures. There was a ghost, a mummy and vampires.

Kathryn Elizabeth Boyles (13)
The Minster School, Southwell

The Roller Coaster

It slowly crept up the tracks. *Click, click, click.*
People had gone silent and their faces spoke for
them. Some with excitement, some horror and
some with mouths hanging open. The machine
was teasing them, gradually curling over the top,
as the people waited for the big drop.

Caitlin Dobb (13)

The Minster School, Southwell

Holiday By The Loch

I was alone, sat by the loch. Blue waters glistened,
the sound of bagpipes drumming down my ear,
until it came towards me. It was less then an inch
away. Its body winding from end to end of the
river. I thought this was only in a myth.

Zoe Beedan (14)

The Minster School, Southwell

Red Liquid

I walked into the house. I saw the kitchen door.
Red liquid came seeping through! *Blood!* I heard
a horrifying scream. I slowly walked towards the
door. I peered through as it creaked, 'Argh!' Oh it
was just my mum spilling a large bottle of red hair
dye!

Charles Stansfield (14)

The Minster School, Southwell

A Day In The Life Of Mr Potato

One day I was planted, warm and comfy in the earth. Wrenched up, carted off, put into a sack. Before I knew it, I was on the shelf, in a trolley and then a shopping bag. Stabbed by a knife, cut into bits, next thing I know, I am chips!

Patrick Mawson (13)

The Minster School, Southwell

Not Alone

Stones crunched under my blistered feet as I ran through the crawling canopy of my island. I knew I was not alone. I stepped into the light and felt the silky sand blanket my feet. I cried into my tattered clothing as I watched another chance at survival sail away.

Sophie Ireland (13)
The Minster School, Southwell

The Dragon's Song

He was walking to the cliff when it happened.
He saw the ancient Taki Raman dragon. Then it
started. The dragon started singing 'The Song of
Dragons'. The man was never seen again.

Christopher Lowe (12)

The Minster School, Southwell

The Man In The Room

The clock ticked, midnight came closer. I stumbled across the pitch-black room. As I did so, I could hear a deep voice singing quietly. I could feel my face burning up as I got closer to the room. I grabbed onto the doorknob and he pulled me in.

Zoë Thurbon (13)
The Minster School, Southwell

Angel Boy

Nothing could be better as they sat on the rock
by the lake. The moonlight shone down, misty on
the water's flawless surface. As the sun began to
rise, he gently slipped away. She wept and wept
and grew cold and waited for the blanket of night
to fall again.

Lizzie Fussey (13)
The Minster School, Southwell

Mini Marvels The East Midlands

Information

We hope you have enjoyed reading this book - and that you will continue to enjoy it in the coming years.

If you like reading and writing, drop us a line or give us a call and we'll send you a free information pack. Alternatively visit our website at **www.youngwriters.co.uk**

Write to:

Young Writers Information,
Remus House,
Coltsfoot Drive,
Peterborough,
PE2 9JX

Tel: (01733) 890066
Email: youngwriters@forwardpress.co.uk